The Legend of CAPTAIN CROW'S TEETH

EOIN COLFER

The Legend of CAPTAIN CROW'S TEETH

Illustrated by Tony Ross

PUFFIN

PUFFIN BOOKS

Published by the Penguin Group
Penguin Books Ltd, 80 Strand, London WC2R ORL, England
Penguin Group (USA) Inc., 375 Hudson Street, New York, New York 10014, USA
Penguin Group (Canada), 90 Eglinton Avenue East, Suite 700, Toronto, Ontario, Canada M4P 2Y3
(a division of Pearson Penguin Canada Inc.)
Penguin Ireland, 25 St Stephen's Green, Dublin 2, Ireland (a division of Penguin Books Ltd)
Penguin Group (Australia), 250 Camberwell Road, Camberwell, Victoria 3124, Australia
(a division of Pearson Australia Group Pty Ltd)
Penguin Books India Pvt Ltd, 11 Community Centre, Panchsheel Park, New Delhi – 110 017, India
Penguin Group (NZ), cnr Airborne and Rosedale Roads, Albany, Auckland 1310, New Zealand
(a division of Pearson New Zealand Ltd)
Penguin Books (South Africa) (Pty) Ltd, 24 Sturdee Avenue, Rosebank, Johannesburg 2196, South Africa

Penguin Books Ltd, Registered Offices: 80 Strand, London WC2R ORL, England

www.penguin.com

First published 2006
1

Text copyright © Eoin Colfer, 2006
Illustrations copyright © Tony Ross, 2006

The moral right of the author and illustrator has been asserted

Set in Baskerville MT by Palimpsest Book Production Limited, Polmont, Stirlingshire
Made and printed in England by Clays Ltd, St Ives plc

British Library Cataloguing in Publication Data
A CIP catalogue record for this book is available from the British Library

ISBN-13: 978-0-141-38130-5
ISBN-10: 0-141-38130-2

For Alessandra

Contents

contents

CHAPTER 1

Baby Talk

My family spend every holiday in a caravan by the sea. All of us get stuffed into a bedroom the size of a car boot. We sleep with the window open. If you have brothers, then you know why.

I myself have four brothers: Marty, Donnie, Bert and HP. Mum says that in ten seconds we can do more damage to the caravan than a hurricane.

You probably think she's exaggerating. You're probably saying to yourself, *they can't be*

1

that bad. Well, they are. Let me tell you a few stories about my brothers. We'll start with the youngest.

Brother 5: HP (Half Pint). You would think that a five-year-old couldn't cause too much trouble, but what HP lacks in size, he makes up for in brains.

One day, on a visit to our little cousin's, HP realized that babies could do whatever they wanted and never get in trouble, so he decided that he would go back to being a baby. So from that day on, for six whole months, HP only spoke in baby talk. We knew he was faking, but Mum and Dad got an awful shock.

Here is a sample conversation.

Dad: Now come on, little guy. What am I holding in my hand? (A banana.)

HP: Mmmm . . . Poo.

Dad: No. Not poo. Think, HP. It's a fruit. Your favourite. It's a ban –

HP: Nana . . .

Dad: Yes! Excellent. You've got it. Nana. Say the whole word now.

HP: Nananana . . . poo.

(At this point Dad puts his head in his hands

and gives up. Donnie and Bert give HP the thumbs up.)

Brothers 4 and 3: Donnie and Bert. I've put them together because they work as a team. Whenever you see one, you can be sure the other is lurking nearby. Bert acts as lookout while Donnie commits the actual crimes.

Mum used to paste sticky labels on stuff Donnie and Bert weren't supposed to touch.

Hands off was stuck on the ice cream.
Do not touch was pasted on the cocoa powder, and . . .
If you open this, you'd better be wearing gloves because I can take fingerprints and I will track you down read the label on the cake tin.

This last message was meant to be a reading lesson as well as a warning. Mum

used to be a teacher.

Mum tried hiding the cake in the cupboard, but Donnie and Bert simply climbed up the shelves like monkeys. In the end, Mum was forced to wrap the biscuits in lettuce leaves and store them in the boot of the car.

Brother 2: Will. That's me. A lovely boy and a real asset to any group. And I'm not just saying that; it's on my school report.

Brother 1: Marty. My older brother. Marty knows the punishment for actually touching a younger brother is a week in his bedroom, so he has to invent other ways to torment us.

Marty usually saves his cruellest tortures for me. He knows I am afraid of ghosts and so plays all kinds of spooky tricks on me. I could fill three notebooks with stories of his nasty pranks.

CHAPTER 2

captain crow's Teeth

We spent the long summer days swimming, building rafts and putting crabs in each other's shoes. The village of Duncade was a great place for a bunch of boys to go on holiday. We had a boat, wetsuits, a tree house and fishing lines. And this year, I had the Sprats' Jig to look forward to.

The Sprats' Jig is a weekly junior-junior

disco for nine to elevens. And even though it has a stupid name, I still couldn't wait to go because I would get to hang around with the big kids. Marty had been a few times the year before and filled my head with images of kids being cool and dancing underneath a spectacular light show. There was even a

rumour that the rock band U2 would be making a special appearance.

The night before the first disco of the summer, I couldn't sleep. This was nothing to do with the disco. This was because Marty was scaring us silly with his favourite ghost story: The Legend of Captain Crow's Teeth.

We were all zipped into our sleeping bags in a room that was only supposed to have two bunks, but Dad had built three more from old planks and hardboard.

Every night, Marty would wait until we were all half asleep, then begin his story. When a person is half asleep he is liable to believe anything. 'Did anyone hear that?' he asked. 'I thought I heard someone outside the window.'

'I didn't hear anything,' I said, even though I knew Marty was pulling our legs.

'Baba,' said HP, who was still doing the baby-talk thing.

Marty switched on his spy torch, shining it on HP. 'Don't try that baby bit on me, HP.'

'Fair enough,' said HP, who was no fool.

'Maybe it was nothing,' continued Marty, shining the light under his own chin, creating spooky shadows. 'Or maybe it was Captain

Crow looking for the boy who planted an axe
in his forehead.'

'Marty,' I said. 'You're scaring the lads.'

'We want to be scared,' objected Bert.

'Yes. And don't leave anything out,' added
Donnie. 'Plenty of blood and guts, please.'

'You asked for it,' said Marty, suddenly switching off the torch, plunging the tiny room into darkness blacker than tar.

He paused for a moment, waiting until we were all good and nervous, then started the story.

'Over three hundred years ago,' he began, in a low wobbly voice, 'the sea around Duncade was terrorized by the dreadful pirate Captain Augustine Crow. Captain Crow was the cruellest, meanest and smelliest pirate ever to set foot on a deck.'

In our minds, Captain Crow looked a bit like Marty, with a beard.

'Crow and his band of pirates lured ships on to the rocks by putting out the lamp in the Duncade lighthouse and lighting another lamp further down the rocks. The ships steered to the starboard side of the pirates' lamp and straight into the reef, where Crow

and his men were waiting. They would loot
the grounded ships, load everything into their
boat, the *Salome*, and sail off to their hideout.
Some nights, when the pickings were
extremely rich, the pirates piled their treasure
high on the rocks that come out of the sea at
low tide. When the pirates' lamp hit those
rocks, they would glimmer and twinkle in the
night like the gold teeth in Crow's own head.

Those rocks became known as . . .'

'Captain Crow's Teeth,' I whispered.

'Wee wee?' said HP.

Marty switched on the torch. 'I'm warning you.'

HP dropped the baby talk. 'I mean, can

you hang on a minute while I go to the bathroom?'

'One minute. Make it snappy.'

HP climbed down from the triple-decker bunks, running off to the caravan's tiny loo. I bet he stopped for a quick hug from Mum to keep him going through the rest of the story.

'One stormy winter night,' continued Marty, when HP was once again tucked into his sleeping bag, 'the *Salome* dropped anchor off Duncade Point. Crow and thirty of his nastiest mates came ashore in rowboats. They were in a mean mood and armed to the teeth with swords, knives and saws.'

'Saws?' asked Donnie. This was new.

'Yes, saws. To cut loose anything they found in the wreckage. Anything, or *anyone*.'

HP shuddered with fear, and the entire bunk-bed system shook.

'The pirates took the lighthouse without

firing a shot, then lit their own signal lamp on another rock. So much buccaneer badness has seeped into that rock that today seagulls won't land on it. And anyone who sits on it gets a cold evil feeling in their bum.'

I rubbed my own bum. It was true. I sat on that rock once for a dare, and had numb-bum for a week afterwards.

'Within the hour, a merchant ship, the *Lady Jacqueline*, came over the horizon and laid a course around Duncade Point – or so they thought. But the light they used for their bearings was the false pirate lamp, and so the pilot ran them aground on the cruel rocks of Duncade.'

It wasn't difficult to imagine, with the wind whispering outside our window and the sea battering the rocks not two minutes' walk away.

'Captain Augustine Crow and his mates

boarded the wreck, howling and waving their
swords, burning fuses smoking in their beards.
They locked the passengers and crew into a

cabin, and stripped the hold of anything they could carry. Crow himself broke down the captain's door, for it was always in the captain's own strongbox that the greatest riches were kept. Inside he found, not the captain, but a cabin boy who had taken shelter in the cabin.

'Crow looked down at him with his black beady eyes and said, "Well, well, well, what does we 'ave 'ere?"

'The boy didn't answer, but instead took his hand from behind his back. In it was a small kindling axe.

'Crow laughed a terrible evil laugh. "Look 'ere, lads," he called to the pirates behind him. "This 'ere infant is going to take on the lot of us."

'While Crow made his joke, the cabin boy swung the little axe. Crow looked back just in time for the axe to sink into the crown of his

head. As he fell to the ground, Crow said,
"Now that's what I call a cabin boy.'"

Marty paused, and nobody said a word.
This was a good sign. If we had been bored,
we would have bombarded Marty with stupid
questions just to annoy him. For example, *Did*

the cabin boy have any pets? No questions meant that everyone was hooked.

'Crow was carried back to the ship by his mates, and the surgeon, who was a butcher by trade, took a look at his wound. "If we take this axe out, the captain's brain will fall out too," declared the surgeon. So they left it in. The ship's blacksmith ground it down until only a sliver of metal remained. It gleamed on the captain's forehead like a half moon.

'Crow woke up after ten days of boiling fever and his first words were, "Where's that boy?" The pirates didn't know. In their haste to rescue the captain, nobody had thought to look for the cabin boy.

'The pirates returned to Duncade, but money could not buy information on the mysterious cabin boy. Captain Crow was furious. Because of this boy, he would have a burning headache for the rest of his life, and he wanted to have his revenge. For the rest of his life, Crow searched far and wide for the boy who had injured him so sorely, and fifteen years later, when the army tracked Crow down to his hideout, his last words before cannon fire blew his stronghold to smithereens were, "I will be back for that cabin boy.""

'How do you know what his last words were?' asked Bert. 'How does anybody know, if his stronghold was blown to pieces?'

Marty was ready for that one. 'There was a survivor. Johnny the Pointer. A pirate with only one finger, who earned his keep by cleaning musket muzzles.'

'Well done,' said Bert, satisfied.

'And so they say, Captain Crow's spirit wanders the headland. And whenever the rocks known as Captain Crow's Teeth glow underneath the water at high tide, his ghost is there, searching for the cabin boy. And if he finds a boy of similar age wandering the rocks in the dead of night, then he will take that boy with him to his ghost ship.'

Bert asked the question that I didn't want asked. 'How old was that cabin boy?'

Marty flicked on the torch, shining it directly into my face. 'He was nine. Will, do you know anybody who is nine years old?'

I swallowed. I did know someone. Me.

CHAPTER 3

The Sprats' Jig

The next day, I quizzed Dad about Captain Crow's Teeth. 'Did you ever see the rocks light up, Dad? Like in the pirate story?'

Dad and I were sitting on the quay wall, fishing for mullet, brown fish that liked to hang around by the mouth of the dock.

Dad wound in his line. 'You know something, Will. I did once, when I was a boy. The whole row lit up exactly like a mouthful of golden teeth just below the surface. Back

23

then, people actually thought that Captain Crow was back, and none of us children were allowed on the rocks, in case we'd be stolen away.'

'Did you go up anyway?' Sometimes kids do things they are not supposed to.

Dad smiled. 'A group of us sneaked over the rocks that very night.'

'Weren't you scared?'

'Scared silly,' admitted Dad. 'To tell the truth, we never made it as far as Captain Crow's Teeth. One of the boys turned and ran, and the rest of us followed him. Imagine, we actually believed that old Captain Crow was over there waiting for us.'

'So what is it then, if it's not Captain Crow?'

'It's phosphorescence,' said Dad.

'Phos-for-whatsits?' I asked.

Dad broke down the word. 'Phos-phor-es-cence. Every now and then, phosphorescent mites are disturbed by the waves and that makes them glow in the dark. It's science; nothing to do with ghosts. But I think I prefer the pirate's teeth explanation.'

Not me. I preferred the science. Scientists

don't jump out of the sea and drag boys back
to their ghost ship.

'How often does this phosphorescence
show up?'

'On those rocks? Hardly ever. I've only
ever seen it happen once.'

Good, I thought. *Hardly ever. And even if it does happen, then it's only science. Nothing to do with pirates, just science.*

Dad grinned. 'Of course scientists don't know everything.'

I swallowed. 'What do you mean?'

'Well, which sounds more realistic? Microscopic creatures that eat sunlight and burp lightning? Or ghostly piles of pirate treasure?'

'Microscopic creatures?' I said hopefully.

'Maybe to you, but I prefer the pirate theory.' Dad opened his mouth wide and laughed a long spooky laugh. 'Ahar, shiver me timbers.'

I knew he was joking, but I didn't think it was funny. No nine-year-old would.

The evening of the big disco had arrived. Marty and I both had showers and put gel in our hair. This was the first time I had ever used gel, and it felt like I was wearing a cap of snails. I wanted to brush it out, but Marty told me it was cool.

'You don't want to be the odd one out,' he said. 'All the other boys will be spiked up. And girls love spiky hair.'

I studied myself in the bathroom mirror. My head looked like someone had glued a terrified cat on to it.

'Are you sure this is cool?'

'Of course it is,' said Marty, adding another dollop to his own head. 'If I'm doing it, then it must be.'

Donnie, Bert and HP were waiting for us when we came out of the bathroom. They laughed so much that the entire caravan shook.

'Poo-poo head,' said HP, in his baby voice.

'This is cool!' I objected.

'Now now, boys,' said Mum. 'Never mind them, Will. Girls love boys who look after their appearance.'

'Will loves girls,' chanted Bert and Donnie, waving their behinds at me, which

was sign language for someone loving girls.

'Mum!' I complained. 'They're waving their bums at me.'

'Get out!' said Mum to my three younger brothers. 'And take those bums with you.'

The boys went, waving all the way.

Mum turned to us. 'Now before you go, you two, sit.'

You two was Marty and me. We squeezed on to one of the seats running along the side of the caravan table. Mum and Dad squeezed in the other side.

'So, the big day has arrived,' said Dad. 'The two sprats are off for a jig.'

Marty put up his hand. 'Pardon me, parents. I got the lecture last year. Can I go?'

'Nope. Some people need to hear things twice.'

'And what's that supposed to mean?'

'Well, how many times have you been told not to eat things off the ground? And you *still* managed to break your tooth on that chewing gum. Do you know how much that cap on your front tooth cost?'

Marty knew when he was beaten, so he

sighed deeply and settled in for the lecture.

'We are placing a lot of trust in you two this evening,' said Mum. 'You are being allowed to cycle somewhere on your own.'

'It's not as if we're going to the end of the world, Mum,' said Marty. 'The dance hall is only down the road from the village. You can see it if you stand on the roof of the caravan.'

'That's not the point,' said Dad. 'I hardly think we're going to spend the evening up on the roof, waiting for you two to come home.'

'And we're not going on our own. There are loads of us going.'

Dad looked at Mum, then at Marty. 'I think we'd better drop you up in the car.'

'No!' squeaked Marty. 'We can't arrive with our parents. That will ruin everything. I'll be grown-up, honest. I'll watch the news on TV before I go. Do you want to talk about the election?'

Dad raised his hands. 'OK. OK. But this is a trial run. The jig is over at ten. I'll give you thirty minutes to get home. If you're not home by then, I'm coming up in the car with your pyjamas, the ones covered in teddy bears,

and I'm making sure everyone sees them.'

Marty's mouth opened in horror. 'You wouldn't!'

Dad smiled. 'Maybe I would, maybe I wouldn't. Let's hope we don't have to find out.'

Mum passed me a sheet of paper torn from her notebook. 'Read this,' she ordered.

I read the words aloud. 'We, Marty and Will Woodman, accept the res . . . respo . . .'

'Responsibility,' said Mum.

'Responsibility, that has been given to us by our won . . . wonder . . .'

'Wonderful parents.'

'Wonderful parents. And if we break either of the following rules, we will be in so much trouble that the happiness we feel at the moment will seem like a beautiful dream.'

'A beautiful dream,' repeated Dad. 'I love

that bit. And what are the rules, Will?'

I read on. 'Rule One: Straight up to the
dance and straight back. No messing about
on the road.'

'Don't you trust us?' said Marty, trying to
look betrayed.

Dad didn't even bother to answer. 'Rule
Two, Will.'

'Rule Two: Stay on the road. Do not set
foot on the rocks.'

'And if you do?'

'And if we do, then the next time we are allowed out our grandchildren will be with us.'

'Is that all?' said Marty. 'Where do I sign?'

'Do you both understand these simple rules?' asked Mum. 'Or do we need to go over them again? Well done, Will, by the way. Lovely reading.'

Marty squirmed with impatience. 'We get the idea. Can we go now? We're going to miss the jig. My hair is going to go flat.'

Mum stood us up before her. 'Right, let me have a look at you.' She inspected us thoroughly. 'Nice teeth. Hair, crazy, but I suppose that's fashion. At least the gel should keep head lice out.'

Dad gave us two euro each. 'For crisps and a drink.'

Marty examined his coins. 'How come Will gets a two-euro coin and I get two one-euro coins?'

'It's all the same.'

'It's not the same. If it was the same, we'd both get one coin.'

'What difference does it make?'

'The difference is that a two-euro coin is better than two one-euro coins,' explained Marty, as though it were obvious.

I wanted to get on the road. 'Here, you take the two-euro.'

Marty scowled at me. 'I can't take it from you. Dad has to give it to me himself, because I'm the oldest.'

Marty was the most stubborn ten-year-old in Ireland. He wouldn't back down even if it meant missing the jig.

I gave the coin to Dad. 'Dad, will you give this to Marty?'

'Anything for a quiet life,' said Dad, flicking the coin to Marty.

Marty slipped the coin into his jeans'

pocket. 'OK,' he said. 'Saddle up. Time to hit the road.'

Our three brothers had prepared a little farewell song for us. They lined up outside the caravan for the performance, and launched into their bum-waving dance as soon as we appeared at the door. 'Will loves girls,' they warbled. 'Will loooves girls.'

HP joined in, goo-gooing the words.

'Why aren't you teasing Marty?' I asked them.

HP whispered in my ear, in case Mum or Dad heard. 'We're not stupid,' he said.

It wasn't true. I didn't love girls. I didn't like dancing much either. I had tried it in the caravan's tiny bathroom and knocked two rolls of toilet paper down the loo. I was only going to the Sprats' Jig because all my friends

were going and I got to stay up late. Maybe I
wouldn't even have to dance.

We mounted our bike and set off up the
lane. We only had one bike between us, and
as the younger brother I was on the back,
perched on a wire carrier.

Marty did his best to cycle through every pothole on the way to the hall. 'Oops, sorry about that,' he called over his shoulder each time. 'I hope that didn't hurt.'

There was nothing I could do but hang on and hope all this bumping wouldn't make me a worse dancer than I already was.

Marty checked the front lamp. 'It'll be dark on the way home. I don't fancy cycling this road in the dark. Who knows what might be hiding in the bushes.'

'Forget it, Marty,' I said. 'You can't scare me with Captain Crow stories. The boys might believe in that stuff, but not me.'

'It's easy to be brave now, when it's bright. Let's see if you believe in Captain Crow later, in the dark.'

Marty really is an expert at scaring people. Even on a sunny summer's evening, he could make me think about later, when it would be dark and I would once again believe in Captain Crow's ghost.

When we arrived at Duncade Hall, there was a crowd inside. I knew most of them. Boys and girls from the village and some of the Dublin holiday crowd. Marty strolled in the door as if he were the disco king, winking at the girls and punching his friends on the arms.

'Where's the light show?' I asked my brother.

'There,' replied Marty, pointing to a purple strip light hanging from the ceiling. It wasn't even turned on.

'That's it!?'

Marty sniggered. 'What did you expect? Super duper laser lights?' All his friends cracked up.

I fumed. Tricked again. When was I

going to stop falling for his fibs?

Suddenly Marty's jaw dropped. 'Look.
U2!'

'Where?' I gasped.

'In your dreams,' said Marty, then laughed
until his jaws ached. 'This is too easy.'

I was not looking as cool as I had hoped, and it was about to get worse. An elderly man climbed up on a little stage and tapped the microphone.

'Evening, sprats,' said the man. It was Mr Watt, the Duncade lighthouse keeper. 'Welcome to the jig. Now, I know some of you are newcomers and you might be a bit shy. So line up for a Paul Jones.'

A Paul Jones? What was a Paul Jones? 'What's a –?'

But that was as far as I got. Marty grabbed my hand and went tearing off down the hall, howling like a demented wolf cub. Someone grabbed my other hand. It was one of Marty's lunatic friends. He was howling too.

'What's a Paul Jones?' I shouted, above the howling and battering of feet.

'We make two circles,' answered Marty's

friend between howls. 'Boys on the outside, girls on the inside. When the music stops, you dance with the girl opposite you.'

Dance with the girl opposite you? I didn't want to dance with a girl.

Mr Watt switched on a little CD player and held the microphone over the speaker. Irish jig music filled the hall.

Marty raced round the outside of the hall, leaping in time to the music. Our human

chain grew longer and longer until every boy had joined in. Inside us, facing out, a circle of girls had formed. And now Marty had caught up with the last boy in our line, so we were in a circle too. Boys going one way, girls going the other. I caught sight of a few other first-timers in the circles. They looked as nervous as I felt.

Mr Watt leaned down near the microphone. 'When the music stops, take your partner by the hand for an old-time waltz.'

We zoomed round until my head spun. Girls flashed by, all teeth and hair. I thought I was going to be sick.

The music stopped. Marty and his friend let go of my hands and darted across to claim their partners. Now I got it! When the music stopped, you danced with whoever was facing you.

I raised my eyes to the girl opposite me.

She was at least a foot taller than I was, and not pleased to be stuck with the new boy.

'What happened to your hair?' she said, pointing to my gelled spikes.

Now, I am one of five brothers, so trading insults is second nature to me. 'What happened to your face?' I asked.

The girl closed her fist and punched me on the shoulder. It was a sore punch. By the

time the sting had died down, she was gone. I ran off to the boys' toilets and hid until the waltz was over.

I emerged from the toilet just in time to be whisked away for another Paul Jones. This time, the girl I ended up with took one look at me and started crying. 'Why me?' she blubbed. 'Why do I always get the weirdos?' She then took a mobile phone from her pocket and called her mother to come and collect her.

In the third Paul Jones, the girl simply pretended I wasn't there. She looked straight through me and sighed deeply. 'Well, I suppose I'll just have to sit this one out,' she said, hurrying from the dance floor.

It seemed as though no one wanted to dance with the new boy. In fact, nobody wanted to dance with any of the new boys. All the nine-year-olds were left without

partners, so we grouped together by the door, praying for ten o'clock. Just a few more Paul Joneses and we'd be free.

No such luck.

At ten minutes to ten, Mr Watt pulled on a black eye patch and growled into the microphone in a TV pirate accent. 'Does we be 'avin' any nine-year-old boys 'ere tonight?' he asked.

Not me, I thought. *I'm not admitting that I'm nine, even to a fake pirate.*

But once again, Marty was on hand to cause trouble. 'Here's one,' he shouted, raising my hand. 'Barely out of nappies.'

I pulled away, but it was too late – I had been spotted.

'Arrr, young Woodman. Come ye to the middle of the floor.'

I didn't want to go, but Marty helped me on my way with a firm push. I stumbled into the middle of a suddenly empty dance floor. I wasn't alone for long. Several other nine-year-olds joined me, betrayed by their brothers or sisters. We huddled together like frightened rabbits surrounded by wolves.

Mr Watt must have noticed that we were

a little afraid, because he switched back to his own voice. 'No need to be frightened, boys. This is just a little bit of fun. Spooky fun!'

Then the normal lights went out and the purple one in the ceiling came on, but it didn't brighten the hall. Instead it picked out huge luminous murals that I hadn't noticed before. The paintings were of bloodthirsty pirates with golden teeth and swords and muskets. They loomed over us, seeming ready to pounce.

The nine-year-olds almost collapsed with fright. The rest of the children cheered wildly.

'We play this game every year with the newcomers,' continued Mr Watt. 'It's a little something we like to call . . .'

'CAPTAIN CROW'S CHOICE!' howled

the other kids, who must have been waiting for this all night.

'That's right,' said Mr Watt. 'Whoever wins this little game will be crowned Captain Crow's Choice, and win a fabulous prize. The rules are simple. Captain Crow has lost something precious to him, and he wants you to find it. But you must do it in the dark. When the music starts, all you nine-year-olds start searching the floor.'

'What are we looking for?' asked the boy beside me.

Mr Watt chuckled. 'Oh, you'll know when you find it. Now, all the older boys and girls sit by the walls and cheer for your favourite.'

'I don't want to play!' I shouted, but the music had already started and nobody heard me. The music was a spooky pirate song that the other children seemed to know by heart.

'Fifteen men on the dead man's chest –
Yo-ho-ho, and a bottle of rum!'

This is not a game, I thought. *This is torture.*

Overhead, the painted pirates seemed to be moving slightly, the hall was vibrating with music and stamping feet, and the nine-year-olds were banging into each other, trying to find whatever it was that Captain Crow was supposed to have lost.

This is crazy, I thought. *I'm getting out of here.*

I dropped to my knees, crawling out from under the group. Apart from the purple light, there was only one other light left on. It was a box with red letters. The letters read E-X-I-T. That was my target. It seemed an awfully long way away.

I hurried across the floor, trying to ignore the old chewing gum that stuck to my hands and the puddles of cola that were seeping through my jeans. Judging by the squeals of delight from behind me, the rest of the nine-year-olds were really enjoying this game, but I didn't want to be Captain Crow's Choice, even when it was just pretend.

The other kids were shouting and squealing, telling the nine-year-olds where to look. But I ignored them. The last thing I wanted to do was to actually find Captain Crow's lost thing.

Keep heading towards the exit, I told myself. *You're nearly there.*

Then my hand landed on something. Or rather *in* something. And the something was chewing my fingers.

'Aargh!' I yelled, jumping to my feet. 'A rat!'

'Aha,' said Mr Watt's voice beside my ear. 'I think we have a winner.'

The lights flicked back on and I saw that there was a set of wind-up dentures clamped to my fingers. The teeth were painted gold.

Mr Watt had been waiting beside the teeth for someone to stumble on to them. He raised my hand like a boxing champion's. 'Will Woodman has found Captain Crow's Teeth. And so he claims the prize!'

Prize. I might as well have the prize. I did find the teeth after all.

Mr Watt pulled me behind him on to the stage. There he opened a toy chest and began dressing me in a pirate costume. First an eye patch and a shirt. Then a toy sword. He tied a black sash round my waist and finished the lot off with a skull-and-crossbones hat.

'Where's my prize?' I asked.

'You're wearing it,' said Mr Watt, out of the side of his mouth. He picked up the microphone again. 'Now, everybody, what

about a big cheer for Will, Captain Crow's official cabin boy.'

Everybody cheered as if I were lucky to be a ghost's cabin boy. I didn't feel lucky at all. What if Captain Crow heard the cheering and came to see what the fuss was about? And if he had to choose a cabin boy, who would it be? The one wearing the pirate costume, of course.

CHAPTER 4

On the Rocks

Marty was waiting for me outside by the bike after the disco. He was not alone. There was a girl sitting on the carrier. My carrier! To my horror I realized that it was the same girl who had punched me on the shoulder during the first Paul Jones.

I pulled on Marty's shoulder until his ear was level with my mouth. 'What's she doing on the carrier?' I whispered. 'Tell her to hoppit. We need to get moving. Ten thirty remember.'

Marty sighed, draping an arm around my shoulders. 'It's like this, Will. The beautiful Margaret has asked me to give her a lift down to the village.'

'But she's a girl,' I hissed. 'We don't want to hang around with girls. And she punched me.'

Marty grinned. 'Really? Wow. I like her.'

'Dad said ten thirty, Marty. Or we'll never get out on our own again.'

'Ten thirty. No problem.'

I was a bit slow catching on. 'Of course it's a problem. You'll never have time to drop Margaret home and then pick me up. We need to get rid of her.'

'What did you say?' said Margaret.

I hid behind Marty. 'Nothing. I was only joking about your face earlier. It's lovely. Honest.'

'You're right,' said Marty. 'I won't have

time to go down and back twice. That's why you have to go home across the rocks and meet me at the gate.'

I chuckled. 'I thought you said I'd have to go home across the rocks.'

Marty grinned. 'Good man. I knew you'd understand.'

I was flabbergasted. 'Marty! Are you mad? I can't go across the rocks. Rule Two: Do not set foot on the rocks. We signed a contract.'

Marty was already on his way to the bike. 'Mum and Dad will never know. You can either stay here and we'll both be in trouble, or nip across the rocks and be home in time.'

I grabbed Marty's arm. 'But what about –'

'Captain Crow? Tell me you weren't just about to say Captain Crow? Don't tell me that you think he's coming for you, just

because you're nine years old and you found
the teeth?'

Of course this was exactly what I had
been about to say. But I couldn't now. 'Of
course not. That's just a silly ghost story. It's
just that the rocks are dark at night. And
there's no moon.'

Marty rolled his eyes. 'OK, Shirley, you can have this.' He took the lamp from his bike and handed it to me. 'And stay on the path.'

That was rich. Safety advice from the very person who was sending me across the rocks.

'Marty, please.'

'What are you worried about? You have a sword, don't you?'

A sword! The toy sword I had won was made of cardboard and wouldn't scare a rabbit, never mind a pirate's ghost. But I knew there was no point in arguing with Marty. Once he made his mind up about something, that was that.

'I'll see you in thirty minutes,' I said, switching on the lamp. 'At the gate.'

Marty mounted the bike. 'You better be there. Because if you're not, I'm telling Dad that you found a girlfriend and you wouldn't come home.'

'That's not fair,' I called after the bike. 'I hate girls.'

'What did you say?' asked Margaret.

'I hate girls,' I shouted, running along the mud path that led to the rocks. 'And you more than all the rest of them put together.'

*

The path along the rocks was a much shorter way home than along the road. But it was also more dangerous. There were crags and pools and shadows that could hide just about anything. And, of course, there were Captain Crow's Teeth. The tide was high that night, so Captain Crow's Teeth should be hidden beneath two metres of water.

I hurried along as fast as I dared. You have to be careful on the rocks, especially at night. Sometimes the seaweed grows right over the path, and if you put one foot in the wrong spot, you could be whisked all the way down to the water. I knew these rocks pretty well, but not well enough to run across them at night. Nobody knows them that well.

With every step I took, I thought about Captain Crow. It was all hogwash; it had to be. I didn't believe in ghosts, certainly not ones with gold teeth hunting for nine-year-old

cabin boys. All the same, I wished I was ten, or even eight. Anything but nine.

I wanted to take off the pirate outfit, but I knew that if I did, it would be the same as admitting that Captain Crow was haunting the rocks. So I left it on, except for the eye patch. Walking along the rocky path with only one good eye would be just stupid.

I knew the name of every rock I passed.

White Stripe, Seagull's Beak and Cod Point. Next were Captain Crow's Teeth. I would walk round the point and nothing would be shining under the water. Absolutely nothing. And even if there was something, it would be phosphorescence. Not pirate's teeth. But there wouldn't be anything. Definitely not.

I trained the bicycle lamp on the path before me. If I kept my eyes on the path, then I wouldn't even see the rocks. Not that it mattered if I did see the rocks. Because they were just rocks. But I wouldn't look. Just in case.

But I did look. I couldn't help it. I allowed my eyes to flick out over the water just for a moment. And that moment was long enough to see the ghostly flash that shimmered beneath the waves. A golden glow. The teeth. I am not kidding. The water shone briefly as though a crescent moon was nailed to the seabed.

I stopped dead.

It couldn't be true. Not possible. All this talk of Captain Crow had my imagination playing tricks on me. I closed my eyes and counted to five.

Goodbye, glow, I thought. *Nice knowing you.*

But when I opened my eyes, the water flashed again, one big crescent made from a million little golden crescents.

'Go away,' I shouted. 'Get lost.'

Ridiculous, I know, shouting at the ocean, but I was willing to give anything a try.

'You're just phosphorescence,' I roared at the glow. 'Nothing to do with teeth, so I'm not scared of you.'

This wasn't true, but I didn't want Crow's Teeth to know that. I was actually terrified. I

stood there in my pirate outfit, trembling slightly. Marty was right. It was a lot easier to believe in ghosts at night.

Keep walking, I told myself.

All I had to do was keep walking. I could already see the lights of Duncade ahead of me. In two minutes I would be in the village; in four minutes I would be in bed.

Walk, I ordered myself. *Walk, you idiot. It's easy. You've been doing it since you were one and a half.*

But I couldn't walk. All I could do was stare at the water, waiting for another flash.

Oh very good. If Captain Crow has come back, then he's going to find you here waiting for him. And if it's phosphorescence, then they'll find you here tomorrow. Frozen stiff. Walk!

So I walked, slowly at first, then picking up the pace. This wasn't so hard. It was all coming back to me. Pretty soon, I might even be able to manage a jog.

'Phosphorescence,' I shouted again, just in case Crow's Teeth hadn't heard me the first time.

I walked on quickly now, trying to ignore the ocean altogether. The flashes had stopped for the moment; maybe they had never been there at all.

As I walked, I muttered complaints to pass the time. 'Stupid Marty and his stupid bike. Stupid Sprats' Jig. Stupid Paul Jones. And stupid Margaret. What happened to my hair? What happened to her face?'

When I ran out of complaints, I distracted myself by singing a song. 'Will loves girls. Will looooves girls.' It was quite catchy really.

I was quite happy singing to myself, when I heard the sound. The sound that I will never forget. It was a terrible moaning, groaning

voice travelling up from the shore.

'Wiiilllllll!'

I tried to pretend that it had only been a noise and not a voice calling my name. Perhaps there was a cow nearby with a wind problem. But then I remembered that there were no cows over the rocks. They might tumble over the limestone shelf.

'Stay back!' I shouted. 'I have a sword!'

The voice called out again and this time it was definitely a voice.

'Wiiiilllllllllllllll!'

And that was definitely my name. Phosphorescence couldn't speak. It was Captain Crow, back for his cabin boy. How could this be happening?

'It wasn't me,' I called into the night. 'I didn't hit you with the axe. This is just mistaken identity.' Ghosts probably didn't care about mistaken identity. One nine-year-old boy was as good as another.

'Anyway, I'm only eight. Honestly.' I had my fingers crossed when I said that.

'Coooommme heeeere, cabin boy.'

Of course, he thought I was a cabin boy. I was dressed like a pirate.

'No, no. You've got it wrong. This is just a costume. Look, this sword is cardboard.' I grabbed the blade and tore it in two. 'See?'

'Youuuuu are my cabin boy. Cooome to meeee.'

I didn't know what to do. The ghost of

Captain Crow wanted to claim me for his ship. I had two choices. I could run away or I could obey the Captain's order. If I ran away, I would probably fall down a blowhole, or else Captain Crow would float after me. If I made him chase me, then he would give me all the hard jobs on the *Salome*. Maybe if I obeyed this first order, he might go easier on me.

'Over heeeere,' called the pirate. 'Hurry.'

'Coming, Captain, sir,' I said. I pointed the bicycle lamp towards the voice, trying to find a shape among the rock shadows. But the blackness swirled around the beam of light like paint, and all I could see was darkness slashed by shelves of rock.

I stepped off the path on to the rock. 'Hello, Mr Captain. How's the head? My mum has loads of paracetemol, if you just let me run home . . .'

'Youuu will never seeee home again. Youuuu are the chosen one.'

For a moment I was more annoyed than scared. Mr Watt and his stupid game. 'That was just a game. Those were wind-up dentures. Joke teeth.'

And right then, a hand shot out of the darkness, through the lamplight and on to my shirt. It was the scariest moment of my life. I was even more scared than the time when I was three and I noticed that my arms

were a bit hairy. Marty told me I was
adopted from a family of monkeys and they
would be coming to take me back any day.

'Get off!' I screamed, pulling away, but
the hand had a tight grip.

'I've been waiting for you,' said Captain
Crow's voice.

I began to babble. 'Sorry I'm late. I was
at the Sprats' Jig. It's a junior-junior disco for
nine to elevens. I went with Marty. We only
have one bike, so I was on the back. Then
they had this thing called a Paul Jones. The
girl is supposed to dance with you, but they
don't if they don't feel like it, but you
probably know all that.'

'Shut up!' shouted Crow. 'You must come
with me, back to the sea.'

Right at that moment, the sea flashed and
sizzled as though underwater fireworks were
being set off.

'Aaah!' squealed Captain Crow, in a much less scary voice. 'The teeth! The teeth!'

Captain Crow let go of my shirt, and his arm disappeared into the darkness. This was very strange.

I heard slapping and grunting noises from below me. It sounded as if Captain Crow was stuck in the rocks. But surely ghosts couldn't get trapped.

'Eh, Captain Crow?' I said timidly. 'Everything OK?'

I strained my ears for an answer, although I wasn't sure I wanted one. After a while I heard a noise, like a small wave breaking or a sigh.

'Will, I need help,' said a voice from the darkness. 'Get me out of here. It's nearly half-past.'

This was strange. Why would Captain Crow be worried about it being nearly half-past ten? There were only two people who needed to be worried about that. One was me, and the other was . . .

I shone the lamp down along the shelf of rock, into the face of the person at the base . . .

'Marty!' I said. 'You're not a pirate.'

For a moment I was delighted, but it

didn't last. I realized what was actually happening, and got really angry really quickly. 'You planned all of this! This is another one of your tricks!'

Marty did look guilty, but there was something else. There was something wrong with his mouth. Something different.

'Oh, Marty! You've knocked off the cap on your front tooth.'

'I know,' said Marty, miserably. 'I swallowed it.'

'Serves you right. Hiding behind the rocks pretending to be Captain Crow. How much did you pay Margaret?'

'Two euro.'

'Two euro? Just to pretend you were dropping her home?'

'Yes.'

I felt like leaving Marty where he was, but I couldn't. He was still my brother, and if we weren't both home by ten thirty, we would both get punished no matter whose fault it was.

I shone the lamp along Marty's body. He
was wedged into a small crevice, with only his
head sticking out. Stuck like a cork in a bottle.
His bicycle lay beside him. He must have
been mad, cycling along the path with no
lights. And all to play a trick on me.

I grabbed his free arm and pulled, not too hard. 'Sorry, you're stuck tight.'

Marty's face turned so pale it glowed in the dark. 'You have to get me out of here. Crow's Teeth are flashing. Didn't you see?'

It's only phosphorescence, I should have said, but I didn't.

'I saw the flash. But you're jammed in there. I'll go and get Dad.'

'Please, Will. Crow will get me. Don't leave me here, we're brothers.'

Marty looked so scared that I couldn't stay mad with him. I took his arm again and yanked until my brother popped from the hole.

We scrambled up the rocky ledge, pulling his bike after us. I clipped the lamp back on the bike, and we hurriedly followed its light to the village. Marty didn't say anything, but checked over his shoulder every few seconds.

He relaxed for a moment when we reached the village, then he began to worry about Mum and Dad.

'I'm dead,' he said. 'Do you know how much that cap cost? And I've lost it.'

I sniggered. 'It's not lost. Actually, you'll probably get it back in a day or two. Maybe you could glue it back on.' I picked up his bike. 'Now come on. We can talk later, if I decide ever to talk to you again.'

For once Marty did what someone told him to do, without argument.

CHAPTER 5

Ten Twenty-Nine and Forty-Eight Seconds . . .

D ad was looking at his watch when we stumbled in the front door. 'Ten twenty-nine and forty-eight seconds.' He looked up at us. 'Oh, boys, you're back. I wasn't expecting you until eleven.'

'Oh ha ha, Dad, very funny,' I said.

Marty didn't say anything because he was hiding his front teeth.

'How was the jig?' Mum asked.

Usually, as the oldest brother, Marty did the reporting, but now it was up to me. 'Awful,' I said. 'I'm never going again. Old Mr Watt expected us to dance with girls.'

'So who did you dance with, Will?'

I glanced over at Marty. Usually he wouldn't waste this chance to tease me, but he had to keep his mouth shut.

'No one special. I think I'll give it a miss next week.'

'And what about you, Marty? Did you have a good time?'

Marty nodded. 'Uh-huh.'

Mum was suspicious. 'That's it? Uh-huh. No complaints? You didn't get into trouble, did you, honey?'

Marty shook his head this time, then stretched in the fashion of a very tired boy.

'Marty's tired,' I explained. 'I think he wore himself out doing the chicken dance. At least that was what he called it. All the other kids laughed so much at him that one threw up. Mr Watt said Marty was the worst dancer he's ever seen. He said that watching Marty trying to dance was like watching a horse trying to ride a bicycle.'

I glared at Marty, daring him to respond, but he couldn't.

Mum closed the book she had been reading. 'Now now, Will. No teasing. Time for bed, both of you.'

Marty scooted off into the caravan's tiny bedroom before he could be asked for a kiss. I followed, dropping my clothes on the floor and climbing into bed.

I tried to sleep, but I couldn't because Marty was twitching and turning in his bunk, shaking the entire bedroom. Eventually I gave up trying, and kicked Marty's bed until he switched on his torch and climbed down.

'What's wrong with you?' I asked.

Marty looked at me as if I were crazy. 'What's wrong? We were nearly grabbed by Captain Crow, and you're asking me what's wrong?'

I hid a smile behind my hand. Marty still thought the flashing underneath the water had been caused by ghosts.

'I saw it, Will. It wasn't my imagination. I was hiding behind the rocks, and when I popped up to frighten you, I saw the Teeth flash.'

'You thought Captain Crow was coming to get you,' I whispered.

'He was.'

A part of me was happy to see Marty getting a taste of his own medicine, but I knew this would haunt him for the rest of the summer holiday.

'Don't you know that flashing is just phosphorescence?'

Marty frowned. 'Phosphor-whatsits?'

'Phosphorescence. Tiny particles that glow when the sea disturbs them. Nothing to do with pirates. Just science. Eejit.'

Marty's eyebrows moved up and down as his brain shifted through disbelief, relief and then annoyance. He scowled. 'You could have told me earlier.'

'I was too busy being frightened by someone pretending to be a pirate.'

He stood to climb into his bunk, then stopped. 'Tonight? When you thought Captain Crow was real? Were you really

scared? Really really?'

'Yes,' I admitted.

'So was I,' said Marty, in a quiet voice for once. 'It feels horrible.'

'Yes, it does,' I said.

Marty held out his hand. 'I'll make you a deal. Because that was a bad one, no more tricks for the rest of the summer.'

I knew a good deal when I heard it.

'Agreed,' I said, shaking the hand.

Marty managed to keep this promise for four whole days, then he convinced me I was going bald. Still, four days was more than I had expected to get.

After Marty had gone to bed that night, I felt myself drifting off to sleep straight away. It was funny, but knowing that Marty had been afraid of Captain Crow's Teeth made me feel better. It was just as Dad had said. Phosphorescence. It hardly ever happens. I was lucky to have seen it.

The next morning, HP gave up the baby talk. He didn't do it on purpose. He did it because he had information too good to waste. HP got up early, as he always did. And, as usual, he draped a dirty sock across everyone's nose, just in case we were still asleep.

When he came to Marty, Marty

half-opened one eye and yawned a huge yawn.

'Yaaaaaarrrrr-r-r-r,' he yawned. Which would have been OK except that he revealed his front teeth. All one and a half of them.

'Marty broke his tooth again!' squealed HP in perfect English. 'Mummy, Daddy, Marty broke his tooth! Do you know how much that cost?'

I jumped out of bed quickly. I couldn't wait to hear how Marty would get out of this one.

MEET
EOIN COLFER

Photograph © Susan Greenhill

What was your favourite book when you were a child?

My favourite book as a child was *Stig of the Dump* by Clive King. A classic.

How did you become a writer?

I think writers are naturally inclined to write stories, just as athletes cannot wait to get out on the sports field. I was helped along by encouragement from my family and teachers.

How did you feel about having four brothers when you were growing up?

Most of the time it felt great to have four brothers. We all stuck up for each other in school and out on the estate.

What tricks did your brothers play on you?

My little brothers were terrible for taking my stuff. Like all little brothers, I suppose. If you had any sweets hidden they could sniff them out. Then again, so could I.

What are your top tips for budding authors?

Read as much as you possibly can and spend the rest of your time writing.

Where do you get your ideas from?

Ideas come from everywhere. Life throws up inspiration all the time, even when you are asleep!

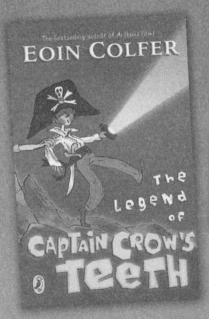

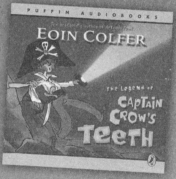